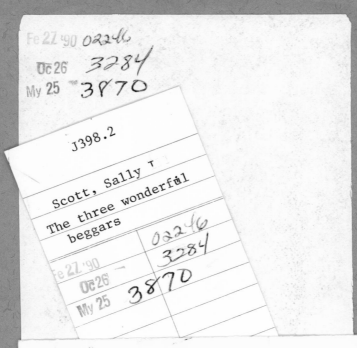

The Three Wonderful Beggars

ADAPTED AND ILLUSTRATED BY

SALLY SCOTT

GREENWILLOW BOOKS, NEW YORK

FOR CAROL AND ROB

Printed in Belgium   First American Edition   10 9 8 7 6 5 4 3 2 1

The story of *The Three Wonderful Beggars* has been adapted from a
version of this Serbian tale in *The Violet Fairy Book* (1901) edited by
Andrew Lang.

Library of Congress Cataloging-in-Publication Data

Scott, Sally.
The three wonderful beggars.

Summary: After predicting that hard-hearted
Mark the Rich will lose his fortune to the
young Vassilil, three beggars save Vassili
from Mark's repeated attempts to kill him.
[1. Folklore]   I. Title.
PZ8.1.S4246Th 1988   398.2′1 [E]   86-22825
ISBN 0-688-06656-9
ISBN 0-688-06657-7 (lib. bdg.)

There once lived a merchant whose name was Mark. He had so much money that people called him "Mark the Rich". But his wealth had made him hard-hearted and if he caught sight of a beggar, he would order his servants to set the dogs on him.

One day, three poor old men came dragging their way to his door. Just as he was about to set the dogs on them, his little daughter begged him to let the poor men sleep for one night in the house.

Her father could not refuse her, and the three were allowed to sleep in the loft.

That night, when everyone was fast asleep, the little girl crept up to the loft and peeped in. The three old men were talking in low voices.

"What news is there?" asked one.

"Ivan in the village has just had his seventh son. What shall we name him, and what fortune shall we give him?" said the second.

"Call him Vassili," said the third, "and give him all the riches of this hard-hearted Mark, who would have driven us from his door."

After a little more talk, the three left the loft and crept softly away.

At that, the little girl, whose name was Anna, ran to her father and told him all she had heard.

The next day, Mark the Rich went into the village to see Ivan.

"Look here, my friend," he said, "you are a poor man, how can you bring up another son? Give him to me and I'll make something of him, and give you a thousand crowns as well. Is it a bargain?"

Ivan scratched his head and thought a bit, but finally he agreed.

Mark the Rich gave him the money, wrapped the baby in a fox skin, and laid it in the sledge by his side. Then he drove off towards his home.

On the way, he pulled up at a cliff and threw the baby over it. "Now try to take my riches!" he said.

Soon after, three merchants were travelling along the same road, on their way to pay Mark the twelve thousand crowns they owed him.

Hearing the sound of crying, they looked over the cliff and saw a little patch of green grass and flowers amid the snow.

Lying among the flowers was the baby.

The three merchants put the baby in their sledge and drove on to Mark's house, where they told him what they had found.

"He's a nice little fellow," said Mark. "I should like to keep him. If you will hand him over to me, I'll forget your debts."

The merchants were very pleased to have made so good a bargain. They left the child with Mark and drove away.

That night, Mark the Rich put the child in a barrel, nailed the lid tight, and threw it into the sea.

The barrel floated a long way on the tide, until at last it drifted close to the shore near a monastery.

The monks were spreading their nets to dry when they saw the barrel. They drew it in to shore, and taking the child home with them, they named him "Vassili".

So the boy lived with the monks, who taught him to read and write and sing, and he grew into a handsome and gentle man.

Now it chanced that Mark the Rich was making a journey in that part of the country, and asked if he might spend a night in the monastery.

The monks showed him their church. It happened that the choir was singing, and one voice, Vassili's, rose above the rest. When Mark asked whose it was, the monks told him Vassili's strange story. Mark knew at once that this was the child he had twice tried to kill.

So he said to the monks: "If you will spare that young man to me, I will make his fortune, and will give you twenty thousand crowns as well."

The monks talked it over, and decided that they could not stand in the way of Vassili's good fortune.

When they had agreed, Mark wrote a letter to his wife, saying:

'When the bearer of this letter arrives, take him to the soap-maker's house, and as you pass the great boiler, push him in.'

Then he gave the letter to Vassili to take to her.

Vassili set out for Mark's house. On the way there he met three beggars, who asked him where he was going.

"I am taking this letter to the wife of Mark the Rich," he replied.

"Show us the letter, Vassili," said the beggars.

He handed them the letter, and before giving it back to him, they each blew upon it, and said: "Now give the letter to Mark's wife. No harm will befall you."

Vassili arrived at Mark's house, and delivered the letter. When Mark's wife read it, she could hardly believe her eyes.

The letter said:

'When you get this letter, make ready for a wedding and let the bearer be married next day to our daughter, Anna.'

Anna saw Vassili, the bearer of the letter, and he pleased her very much, and so the next day he was given fine clothes and the wedding took place.

When Mark the Rich returned home, and found that Vassili was now his son-in-law, he flew into a rage. But his wife showed him the letter which Vassili had brought her, and there were his orders plainly written in his own handwriting. There was nothing to be done.

Then one day Mark the Rich said to Vassili, "I want you to go to my friend the Serpent King. Twelve years ago he built a castle on some land of mine. I want you to ask him for the rent, and you must find out what he has done with the twelve ships I sent him long ago."

Vassili said goodbye to his young wife, who cried bitterly at parting, and set out.

One day Vassili was tramping along when he heard a voice ask: "Where are you going?"

"Who spoke?" said Vassili.

"I did," said a very old oak. "Tell me where you are going."

"I am going to the Serpent King."

"When the time comes," said the oak, "ask this of the King: 'Rotten to the roots, half dead but still green, stands the old oak. Is it to stand much longer on earth?'"

"Very well," said Vassili. He continued on his way until he came to a river. There a ferryboat was waiting, and Vassili jumped in.

"Are you going far, my friend?" asked the ferryman.

"I am going to the Serpent King," Vassili replied.

"Then say to the King: 'For thirty years the ferryman has rowed to and fro. Must he row much longer?'"

"Very well," said Vassili, "I'll ask him."

Vassili walked on and on, until at last he reached a narrow arm of the sea, across which lay a great whale. People walked and rode over its back as though it were a bridge.

As he stepped onto the whale, it said to him: "Do tell me where you are going."

"I am going to the Serpent King," Vassili replied.

"Then say to the King," said the whale: "'The poor whale has been lying for three years across an arm of the sea, and men and horses have nearly trodden his back into his ribs. Is he to stay there much longer?'"

"I will," said Vassili, as he stepped off the whale's back onto the other shore.

He walked on and on, until at last he came to a large castle built of marble, shining in the sunlight.

Vassili walked into the castle and through the rooms. In the last room there was a beautiful girl.

"O Vassili!" she cried, "whatever brings you to this place?"

Vassili told her why he had come, and what he had seen and heard on the way.

"You have not been sent here for the rent at all," said the girl, "but only that the Serpent may eat you."

She had no time to say more, for the castle shook and a hissing sound was heard.

The girl pushed Vassili into a chest and said: "Listen carefully to everything the Serpent and I say."

The next moment the Serpent King rushed into the room, and the girl rose to greet him.

"I've flown half over the world," he cried, "and I'm very tired and want to sleep. Scratch my head."

The girl sat down near him, stroked his ugly head, and said in a coaxing voice: "You know all that can be known in the world. Will you tell me the meaning of this dream?"

"Out with your dream, but be quick," said the Serpent.

The girl began: "A man was walking on a wide road, when an oak tree said to him: 'Ask this of the King, rotten to the roots, half dead but still green, stands the old oak. Is it to stand much longer on earth?'"

"It must stand until someone comes and pushes it down with his foot," said the Serpent. "Under its roots he will find more gold and silver than even Mark the Rich possesses."

Then the girl repeated the ferryman's question.

"If someone gets into the boat to be rowed across," said the Serpent King, "the ferryman has only to push the boat off and go on his way without looking back, and the man in the boat will have to take his place."

Next the girl told him what the whale had asked.

"He will have to lie there until he has thrown up the twelve ships of Mark the Rich," said the Serpent. "Then he can plunge into the deep sea and his back will be healed."

And with that, the Serpent King closed his eyes, turned on his side and snored until the windows rattled.

As soon as the Serpent was sound asleep, the beautiful girl helped Vassili from his hiding place and showed him the way home. He thanked her with all his heart, and set off.

When he reached the whale, it asked:

"Have you thought of me?"

"I will tell you what the Serpent King said as soon as I've reached the other side," Vassili replied.

"Now," said he, when he was safely on the opposite bank, "throw up those twelve ships of Mark the Rich that you swallowed three years ago."

The great animal heaved himself about and threw up the twelve ships and all their crew. Then he shook himself for joy, and plunged into the sea.

Soon Vassili came to the ferry.

"Take me across," he said to the ferryman, "and I will tell you what you want to know."

"Now," said he, safe on the other shore, "when the next man comes along and wants to be taken across, you must step ashore and push him off in the boat. Then you will be free, and the other man must take your place."

When Vassili came to the oak tree, he pushed it with his foot and it fell over. Under its roots lay more gold and silver than even Mark the Rich possessed.

Just then, the twelve ships came sailing up the river. They cast anchor and the sailors took the gold and silver on board. Then they set sail for home with Vassili.

Mark the Rich was furious to see Vassili return. He jumped on his horse to ride to the Serpent King and find out why the lad had not been eaten.

When he reached the river he sprang into the ferry. The ferryman stepped ashore and pushed the boat out into the river.

Now it is Mark the Rich who plies the ferry. His face is wrinkled and his hair is white.

As for Vassili, he never turned a beggar from his door, and lived a happy life with his good and gentle wife, Anna.